y
Adler, David A.
Eaton Stanley and the
mind control experiment

EATON STANLEY
AND THE
MIND CONTROL
EXPERIMENT

EATON STANLEY AND THE MIND CONTROL EXPERIMENT

◆◆◆◆◆◆◆◆◆◆◆◆

DAVID A. ADLER

ILLUSTRATED BY JOAN DRESCHER

E. P. DUTTON NEW YORK

Library of Congress Cataloging in Publication Data

Adler, David A.
  Eaton Stanley and the mind control experiment.

  Summary: Two sixth-grade boys try to control their
teacher's mind, but find their project getting out
of hand when serious things start happening to her.
  1. Children's stories, American. [1. Schools—
Fiction] I. Drescher, Joan E., ill. II. Title.
PZ7.A2615Eat 1985 [Fic] 84-21135
ISBN 0-525-44117-4

Published in the United States by E. P. Dutton, Inc.,
2 Park Avenue, New York, N.Y. 10016

Published simultaneously in Canada by
Fitzhenry & Whiteside Limited, Toronto

Editor: Julie Amper   Designer: Edith T. Weinberg

Printed in the U.S.A.   W   First Edition
10 9 8 7 6 5 4 3 2 1

to my parents-in-law
with love

ONE

◆◆◆◆◆◆◆◆◆◆◆

The first time I saw Eaton Stanley, I should have kept right on walking. He was sitting on the ground with his legs crossed, waiting for the school bus. I should have walked to school that day. But I didn't. I stood and waited near the corner, just a few steps from Eaton.

"Did you know you can't keep your eyes open when you sneeze?"

It was Eaton. He was talking to me.

"I said, did you know you can't sneeze with your eyes open?"

"No."

"Well, you can't. And mice don't love cheese. They'd rather eat seeds, meat or vegetables."

By the time the bus came, I knew the exact weight of a basketball and the number of feathers on a pelican's back.

Eaton sat next to me on the bus. He really loves to talk. He told me that he and his father had just moved into the Bakersville Apartments. His parents are divorced, and his mother is too busy to take care of him. She travels all over, selling jewelry. Eaton's father is an accountant. When he told me that, Eaton rolled his eyeballs up and said "Boring." I guess it is.

"I read encyclopedias," he said.

"What?"

"When I'm bored, I read encyclopedias. Right now I'm up to *polyphony*. It's in the middle of volume fourteen."

That's when I rolled *my* eyeballs up and said "Weird." Then I asked Eaton what *polyphony* is.

"It's some kind of music," he said. "Bach wrote a lot of it."

The bus had to wait for Alice Brenner. It happens just about every day. Alice's mother comes outside and tells Mr. Ellman, he's the driver, that Alice is almost ready. Mrs. Brenner stands there to make sure the bus doesn't leave. Then Alice runs out drinking soft-boiled eggs from a paper cup. When she gets to the bus, she takes one last big swallow and gives her mother the cup. A whole bunch of us, mostly the boys, cheer when she gets on the bus. Not because we're glad to see her —we're just glad we don't have to wait any longer.

While we were waiting, Eaton told me his name. "It's horrible, isn't it?" he asked. "Every time I get a new teacher, she thinks that Stanley is my first name and Eaton is my last."

"Well, my name is Brian Newman," I said.

"Now that's a name," Eaton told me. "No one would ever think of calling you Newman Brian."

When we stopped at the traffic light, Eaton told me

2

that traffic-light bulbs should last at least eleven months. The poles should last fifteen years. Goldfish live longer than guppies, and fingernails grow about one inch every fifteen months.

Most kids get to school early enough to play in the yard for a while. We don't. We waste too much time waiting for Alice. Just as we got off the bus, the first bell rang. I asked Eaton what class he was in.

Eaton showed me his yellow card with his room and teacher assignment. When I saw Eaton waiting for the bus, I should have kept right on walking. And when I saw that yellow card, I should have gone straight to the principal and asked to have my class changed. But I didn't.

"Come with me," I said. "You have Mrs. Bellzack. We're in the same class."

We're on the fourth floor, all the way in the back of the building. I think the principal puts us and the other older kids there to keep us away from his impressionable kindergarten and first-grade classes. I don't mind. It also means we're far away from the principal. There's no elevator in the building, and he's too lazy to walk up three flights of stairs, so we hardly ever see him.

The halls were noisy and crowded. Eaton looked around as he walked. In the first-floor stairwell, there are posters telling us to drink milk, brush our teeth and get plenty of sleep. The second- and third-floor posters tell us to read. On our floor the message is "It's cool not to smoke."

Eaton wasn't watching where he was walking. He was trying to see the whole school at once. He bumped into Mrs. Cannon.

"Don't you say 'Excuse me,' young man?"

Eaton said, "Excuse me, young man." Only he said the *young man* part in a whisper.

"That's mean Mrs. Cannon," I said after she'd gone. "I had her last year."

"Well, come on then," Eaton said. "Let's meet lucky Mrs. Bellzack. Then he looked at me, smiled and said, "She's lucky because today she gets a bright new student. Me."

TWO

◆◆◆◆◆◆◆◆◆◆◆

When we came into the room, Mrs. Bellzack was writing a math assignment on the board. She teaches us everything except science. Ms. Stanton teaches us that. While we waited for Mrs. Bellzack to finish writing, Eaton looked around the room.

On one wall Mrs. Bellzack has a sign that says Top Tests. One of the math tests under that sign is mine. I got a ninety-three. And there are a few newspaper articles about Benny Hunt, a college basketball player. Right over the articles Mrs. Bellzack wrote, *Benny Hunt, star athlete, brother of our own Jenny Hunt.* Jenny sits right behind me, but she's not much of a star. She always pokes me during tests and asks to look at my paper.

On the back bulletin board, Mrs. Bellzack has what she calls her Creativity Wall. It's covered with drawings, paintings and essays. I don't have anything up there.

The other kids came in and sat down. I saw Eaton look them over. I don't know what he was looking for. Maybe he knows some statistic about the average number of boys in a class or how many brown-haired boys wear green shoes, and he wanted to see how we fit in.

I left Eaton by Mrs. Bellzack's desk. I figured he could handle himself. I sat down and began to copy the assignment from the board.

Eaton gave Mrs. Bellzack his yellow card. She looked at it and said, "Well, Stanley Eaton, welcome to our class."

When Mrs. Bellzack said that, Eaton looked at me and rolled his eyeballs up.

"It's Eaton Stanley," he told her. "Eaton is my first name."

"Oh, I'm sorry. Now just a minute." She wrote Eaton's name in the roll book. Then she gave Eaton a home contact form and book receipt cards.

"Fill these out and give them back to me." She pointed to the row of seats next to the window and said, "You can sit in the last seat."

During class, Eaton didn't say much. I thought his hand would be up all the time. When Mrs. Bellzack asked us about President Calvin Coolidge, I was sure he would tell us Calvin's height, weight, the color of his eyes and his favorite vegetable. But he didn't.

Eaton was quiet during math too. But what can you say about the square root of nine? It's three and that's it.

Just before science Mrs. Bellzack told us that each sixth-grade class would be doing a senior project. We had to decide how to raise some money. The money would be used to buy the school a gift. That's when

Eaton's hand went up. But so did lots of other hands.

"Yes, Janet."

"I could bake chocolate chip cookies and sell them. And we could buy the school an elevator."

"Daniel."

"What about if we washed cars? And I don't know what we could do with the money."

"Susan."

"We could give the school a year's supply of paper towels. We never have any in the bathrooms, and I hate walking around with wet hands, especially when it's cold out."

"Eaton."

"We could make up history birthday cards. People would tell us what day the birthday is, and we would make up a card with a list of what happened on that date."

"That's a very interesting idea, Eaton."

"Like, for example, I was born on April the 10th. That's the day the safety pin was invented. Well, not really invented. It's the day it got its patent."

My eyeballs rolled up. We had science in less than ten minutes, and I didn't think Eaton would be through by then.

"April the 18th would have been a good day to be born, too. That's when the first laundromat was opened. And it's when Paul Revere made his famous ride to warn the colonists that the British were coming."

"I think we get the idea, Eaton."

"We could use the money we earn to buy the front

pages from old newspapers, like one from July 21, 1969. It was the morning after the first moon walk, and the headline was U.S. Walks on Moon. If we had lots of different newspapers framed and hung them in the lobby, it would really teach everyone a lot about history."

"Well, thank you very much, Eaton. Why don't we all think about our senior project. Maybe some of you will have other ideas. Now get your books together. It's time for science."

When we went to Ms. Stanton's room, Eaton walked next to me.

"How could she say We'll think about it? Did you hear those other ideas? Do you know how many cookies we'd have to sell to buy an elevator? And who ever heard of giving a school paper towels? Those kids in our class are real ping-pongs."

"Ping-pongs?"

"Yeah, you know, bouncy and jumpy, but nothing inside."

Ms. Stanton's lesson was on minerals. Something can be a mineral if it was never alive. Coal comes from plants and trees, so it's not a mineral even though lots of people think it is.

After class, Ms. Stanton spoke to Eaton. She told him about the science project we all have to do. She lets us do it on anything we want. I'm making an incubator. When I'm done, my father will get some fertile eggs from a farm, and I'll see what happens.

On the way back from science, Eaton told me, "I'm steamed at Bellzack. Ideas are worth money, and that idea I gave her about the birthday cards is a good one. She better not listen to those ping-pongs. I'm the guy with a paddle in his hands."

"What?"

"If you had any brains, would you be a Ping-Pong ball or the paddle that hits it?"

"The paddle."

"And that's what we are," Eaton said. "Paddles."

Eaton sat quietly in Mrs. Bellzack's class. He just stared straight ahead.

Eaton walked with me to the bus. He didn't say anything while the bus stood there in front of the school. I remember thinking that it must be hard for someone like Eaton to keep quiet for so long. Then, when the bus started to move, he spoke.

"I know what I'm doing for Ms. Stanton's science project," he said. "I'm going to experiment with mind control."

"With what?"

"I'm going to try to take control of someone else's mind."

"Whose?"

"Mrs. Bellzack's."

THREE

◆◇◆◇◆◇◆◇◆◇◆

I looked at Eaton. I couldn't tell if he was kidding. He looked serious.

"But you can't control someone else's mind," I said.

"How do you know? Maybe I can. That's what will make this a real experiment. We really don't know what will happen."

I looked out the bus window for a while. We passed the drive-in cleaners, the drive-in bank teller and the doughnut drive-in. There must be people in my neighborhood who never leave their cars.

Then I turned to Eaton and asked, "But why Mrs. Bellzack?"

"She's the perfect person," he said with a smile. "She stands in front of the class and talks to us for hours each day. It will be easy to tell if I have any control over her."

Eaton didn't say anything more about his experiment. He told me about his new apartment. He had just moved two days before. Most of his clothing, his books and his collections were still packed in boxes. He has collections of shells, ballpoint pens, old postcards, menus and candy wrappers. Eaton told me I could see them when they were unpacked. He said I was the only kid in the class he would show them to —because I'm not "vacant" like the others. Being vacant is like being a ping-pong.

When I got home, my brother Mark was already there. He's in high school, and he gets out earlier than I do. He was eating, as usual.

"Hey, Brian, you want some?" It was peanut butter on lettuce.

"No thanks. I'll wait for supper."

I went to my room to work on my incubator. I had everything I needed—two cardboard boxes, some old newspaper, a thermometer, a dish for water, a light with a cord and some clear heavy plastic. The plastic was the hardest thing to get. I took it off a see-through box of chocolate-covered doughnuts. Mark said that without the plastic, the doughnuts would go stale. So he ate them.

I took a pair of scissors from the sewing kit and made a window in the bigger of the two boxes. While I worked, I thought about Eaton. *He's weird, but interesting,* I thought. I wondered if he really could take control of Mrs. Bellzack's mind. It would be great if he could. I'd make him get me better grades. Maybe even the sixth grade math award.

I stapled the plastic to the window of my incubator. I put the newspaper, water dish and thermometer inside the smaller box. I put that box inside the bigger

one so that the opening faced the window. I looked through it. It was easy to see the thermometer.

While Mark was putting the lamp into my incubator, I asked him if he knew anything about mind control.

"I don't believe in that stuff," he said.

I waited for him to tell me more, but he didn't. He finished hooking up the lamp, turned it on and went back to the kitchen.

The next morning on the bus, Eaton said he would need my help. "I need someone objective to keep a record of the effect my experiment has on Mrs. Bellzack."

"But I don't know anything about mind control."

Eaton gave me a small notebook and said, "This will be the experiment logbook. You just write what happens."

"I don't know anything about mind control," I told him again.

"You know, there's no one else I would trust with this." Then he looked out the window and said, "Can you believe that Alice. She's late again."

I leaned over Eaton and looked out. Mrs. Brenner had one foot in the street and the other on the first step of the bus. She knew Mr. Ellman couldn't drive off with her standing that way. As Alice ran out of the house, her notebook fell. Papers flew out onto the front lawn of her house.

"We can't wait anymore," Mr. Ellman said.

"It will only take another minute," Mrs. Brenner

told him as she watched Alice run to grab the flying papers.

It took more than a minute, but Mrs. Brenner didn't take her foot out of the bus, so Mr. Ellman waited. When Alice got on the bus, she was pushing papers into her notebook.

"Because of you," one boy said, "I got in trouble for being late."

A few other kids complained. But Alice didn't answer them.

"Nothing will happen until after lunch," Eaton whispered to me as we walked into the building. "Bring the logbook to the cafeteria, and I'll show you what to do."

Just before lunch Mrs. Bellzack asked if there were any new suggestions for our class project. No hands went up.

"I thought Eaton's idea was a good one," Mrs. Bellzack said. "How many of you are in favor of making history birthday cards?"

At least twenty hands went up. "Well, that's what we'll do," Mrs. Bellzack said. Then she told us to line up for lunch.

I took my lunch bag and the logbook and waited in line outside the classroom. Mrs. Bellzack waited with us. Eaton was the last to come out of the room. He looked at me and smiled.

I always ate with Barry and Avi. When I told them I was sitting with the new boy, they looked insulted, but I couldn't help it. I knew Eaton wouldn't talk to me about his experiment with them around.

Between bites of his cream-cheese sandwich, Eaton told me, "Last night I cut pictures from magazines. I pasted them on a large sheet of paper and made a collage of a woman. Her head is bigger than it should be, but that will help us with the experiment."

Eaton took another bite of his sandwich. He drank some milk. Then he went on.

"While you and the others were out in the hall, I tacked the collage onto the Creativity Wall. It's at eye level, just opposite Mrs. Bellzack's desk. I hope she leaves it there."

"What will happen?"

"I just want her to notice it today. If she does, then tomorrow the experiment goes into stage two. Now, open the logbook."

I opened it. Something was already written on the first page.

Experiment:
Object: To gain some measure of control over the mind of an adult subject.
Procedure: Subject will be encouraged to identify with a changing object.
Subject: Mrs. Bellzack.

"Turn the page," Eaton told me. "That's where the log begins. There's a space for you to write what happens today."

I turned the page.

16

Day 1.
Procedure: Large collage of woman placed at eye
level on wall directly opposite subject.
Object: To capture subject's attention.
Results:

Eaton told me to fill in the *Results* part.

As soon as we went back to class, I looked at the back bulletin board. It would be hard to miss Eaton's collage. He had pasted it on a large sheet of glossy blue paper. The woman had lots of hair. It looked like Eaton had used the hair from several pictures in women's fashion magazines. The face itself was all from one picture, but it was obvious that the woman's body had been cut from another picture. It was much too small for the face. Eaton had pasted two large hands onto the collage. They were placed palms up, as if the woman was begging for money or something.

Mrs. Bellzack was still in the hall. When everyone was in the room, she came in and closed the door. She went to her desk to get some papers. Then she looked up. She looked over our heads at the back bulletin board.

She noticed the collage. I'm sure she did because she looked there for a real long time.

FOUR

◆◇◆◇◆◇◆◇◆◇◆

Mrs. Bellzack had this funny look on her face, as though she didn't know what the collage was. Maybe she was wondering how it got there. After what was probably just a few seconds, even though it seemed like more, Mrs. Bellzack began the math lesson. It was on multiplying fractions.

"This is a pie," Mrs. Bellzack said. She drew a circle on the board. In math, teachers love to draw circles and call them pies. To me they look like circles.

"Now I'm going to cut this pie into fourths," she said, and she drew two lines in the circle. She shaded in one section of the pie.

"This is one-fourth of the pie. If we multiply one-fourth by three, what do we get?"

I raised my hand. While I waited to be called on, Jenny Hunt tossed a folded note on my desk. Barry smiled. The note was from him.

"Lana," Mrs. Bellzack said.

"One-fourth multiplied by three equals three-fourths."

I opened the note. "What flavor pie is that," the note said, "blueberry, apple or cherry?"

I rolled my eyeballs up. *How dumb,* I thought. Then I crushed the note and put it in my desk. I didn't want Eaton to see it and think my friend Barry was a ping-pong.

Mrs. Bellzack wants us to understand what we're doing in math. She makes a big deal about it. I wish she wouldn't. She spent forty minutes teaching us how to multiply fractions, and all you have to do is multiply the top by the top and the bottom by the bottom. One-fourth times one-half equals one-eighth because one times one is one and four times two is eight.

Math could be real easy if teachers didn't draw so many pies. If they would just tell us what to do, we'd save a lot of time.

On the bus going home, I asked Eaton what he wanted me to write in the logbook. He told me that we'd talk when we got off the bus.

Alice Brenner has a bus stop right in front of her house, but for the past few afternoons, Mr. Ellman hadn't been stopping there. First he stopped one house past Alice's house. Then he began stopping two and three houses away. I knew he was doing it because he was angry at Alice for making him wait in the morning.

Well, since Eaton wasn't talking, I looked out the bus window. I saw a woman standing in front of Alice's house, right in the middle of the street. She was

19

waving her arms, signaling the bus to stop. She was Alice's mother. Mr. Ellman stopped the bus. He had to. Alice went to the door, but Mr. Ellman didn't open it. I think he was waiting for Mrs. Brenner to move out of the street so he could drive a little further before he let Alice out. But Mrs. Brenner didn't move. Mr. Ellman looked at his watch, muttered something and then opened the door.

When we got off the bus, Eaton said, "We can't talk about the mind control experiment on the bus or anywhere that people from school can hear you. I don't want anyone telling Mrs. Bellzack what we're doing."

I looked around. There was no one nearby. "What do I write in the logbook?" I whispered.

"Write what happened."

"But nothing happened," I said. "Mrs. Bellzack just looked at the collage."

"Then that's what you write. And anyway, that's what I wanted her to do. The experiment is just beginning."

As we walked home, Eaton was his old self again. He was talking about everything. He told me that Yugoslavians love to walk and their flag is red, white and blue, with a little gold in it.

"How do you know that?" I asked. "You've only read up to *p* in the encyclopedia, and Yugoslavia starts with a *y*."

"I know lots of things," he said, "like teachers live longer than writers, and centipedes don't have one hundred legs—they have a lot less."

I wondered about Eaton. Did he make up all that

20

stuff about centipedes, traffic lights and Yugoslavians? How could anyone know so much? He's strange all right, but kind of interesting too. And I was excited by his experiment. I wondered what would happen.

When I got home, Mark told me that Dad had left some things for me on my bed. I saw them as soon as I came into my room. Dad had bought the fertile eggs, twelve of them. I carried the eggs real carefully and put them inside my incubator. Then I turned on the light.

I looked through the window at the eggs. Every three days I planned to take out one egg and crack it open. That way I could watch how a chicken grows inside the egg. Any eggs that would be in the incubator for three weeks should hatch.

While we waited for the bus the next morning, Eaton told me that from then on, he would only talk to me about his experiment after I wrote my notes in the logbook. "I won't tell you what I'm doing," he said. "And I won't tell you what's going to happen to Mrs. Bellzack. I don't want to influence what you write in the log. That would ruin the experiment."

When we came to class, I looked at the back bulletin board. The collage hadn't changed. All through class I wondered what Eaton would do next with his experiment.

At lunchtime, Eaton stayed behind again. I sat with Barry and Avi. I was already eating the second half of my tuna-fish sandwich when Eaton showed up. "You may be eating a dolphin," he said as he unwrapped his sandwich.

"What?"

"Sometimes dolphins get caught in the tuna nets."

I looked at my sandwich. Then I took a bite. It was tuna fish all right. I know the taste.

"And those potato chips you're eating," Eaton said to Barry, "did you know that raw potato leaves are poisonous?"

Avi quickly pushed the licorice he was eating into his mouth.

"You don't know everything," I told Eaton. "Maybe that cream cheese you're eating is made from goat's milk."

"Oh, I hope so," Eaton said. "Goat's milk is very healthy."

While I was walking back to class, Barry whispered to me, "I'm not sitting near Eaton anymore. He takes the fun out of eating."

"That goes for me too," Avi said.

In class, the first thing I did was look at the collage. The hair had changed. It was all blonde. The same color as Mrs. Bellzack's.

FIVE

◆◆◆◆◆◆◆◆◆◆◆

I took out the logbook and wrote:

> *Procedure: Collage woman's hair is blonde now, just like Mrs. Bellzack's.*

I didn't write the *Results* part because nothing had happened yet.

Mrs. Bellzack came into the room. She sat at the edge of her desk, like she does when she wants to talk to us. Then she saw the collage. This time she *really* looked at it. Then she started to talk to us about our senior project, the history birthday cards. I took out the logbook and wrote:

> *Results: Mrs. Bellzack looked at the collage for a long time.*

"If we want to start our senior project," Mrs. Bellzack said, "we'll have to divide the work. First we'll need posters to advertise the cards."

"I'll make some posters," Janet said.

"So will I," Susan said, "but how much will each card cost? I think we have to put that on the poster."

Eaton raised his hand. I had the feeling he had this card business all figured out and was going to tell us just what to do. I was right.

"First of all," Eaton said, "we'll charge a dollar for each card. I've made a study of birthday card prices."

My eyeballs rolled up. I knew we were in for a long lecture.

"Some machine-made cards cost more than a dollar, so it isn't too much for a handmade, personalized card. Then we have to have a sample card on each poster. And the posters have to be in stores and on lampposts, not just in the school."

"Very good suggestions," Mrs. Bellzack said. "Let's give some of the others a chance."

We talked for a long time about the cards, and Eaton had his hand raised the whole time. Whenever Mrs. Bellzack gave him a chance to talk, he went on and on. In the end, Mrs. Bellzack divided the class into committees. There was a committee to make posters and sell the cards and one to do the research. There was a committee to make the cards and one to deliver them. Eaton and I were on the research committee.

Eaton told the card committee some things that happened on April 10th so they could make a few sample cards. April 10th is Eaton's birthday.

On the bus after school, Eaton said, "I hope someone buys a birthday card for November 4th. That's the day Abraham Lincoln was married."

I asked Eaton what they ate for dinner at the wedding. I was only joking.

"Probably chicken," Eaton said. "Chicken and rice."

It's hard to joke with Eaton.

I waited until we got off the bus to ask Eaton about his experiment. He wouldn't talk about it. He just kept talking about Lincoln's wedding.

"They might have had ice cream for dessert. Did you know that some people say that the first ice cream was made when someone left milk out in the cold? But I think all he made was cold milk. People in the United States eat more ice cream than anywhere else in the world. The most popular flavor is vanilla."

"Enough!" I told Eaton. I was glad it was Friday. I couldn't take much more of Eaton telling me things.

When I got home, I looked at my eggs. They hadn't changed, but I knew a chicken was growing inside each one. I checked the thermometer. The temperature was 103° Fahrenheit. Just right.

On Sunday it was time to crack open one of the eggs. But I didn't really want to see a three-day chicken embryo. I didn't want to kill such a young chicken. I figured that I could look at a four-day or a five-day embryo instead. So I left all the eggs in the incubator.

Monday morning at the bus stop, Eaton was carrying a large cream-colored envelope. I asked him what was inside. Eaton wouldn't tell me, so I figured it had something to do with the experiment.

When we got to Alice Brenner's house, Mrs. Brenner ran outside. She put her foot on the first step of the bus and smiled at Mr. Ellman. He didn't smile back.

"You can't keep holding up this bus," Mr. Ellman said.

"Alice is almost ready."

Almost took six and a half minutes. I timed her. Alice ran out holding her paper cup of soft-boiled eggs. She drank the eggs as she ran to the bus.

In the morning, all through class, I wondered what Eaton would do to the collage. He came late to lunch again, so I knew he had done something.

After lunch, as soon as I walked into the room, I looked at the collage. The woman had eyeglasses now. And she was wearing a green dress. Eyeglasses and a green dress might not seem like a big deal, but they were. The glasses had thin brown frames, just like the ones Mrs. Bellzack wears. And that day Mrs. Bellzack was wearing a green dress.

Eaton was making the collage woman look more and more like Mrs. Bellzack. But I didn't know why.

Mrs. Bellzack was making a chart on the board. It listed all the countries in Eastern and Western Europe, their capitals, forms of government, populations and industrial products. Above the chart, Mrs. Bellzack had written *Copy into your notebooks.*

I took out the logbook and wrote:

Procedure: The collage woman has eyeglasses and a green dress, just like Mrs. Bellzack.

27

I left the *Results* part blank because nothing had happened yet.

I took out my notebook and began to copy the chart. *It's going to take at least an hour to copy this,* I thought. I was sure that Mrs. Bellzack just wanted to keep us quiet.

I was copying the forms of government when Mrs. Bellzack finished writing. She put the chalk down and walked to her desk. Then she stopped. She saw the collage. She stared at it. I wondered why she didn't say anything, ask us whose collage it was. But she didn't. And none of the kids in the class asked about it either.

Mrs. Bellzack stared at the collage for what seemed like a long time. Then she looked away and went to her desk. I took out the logbook and wrote the results:

Mrs. Bellzack really looked at the collage, like she was looking in a mirror.

After we finished copying the chart, Mrs. Bellzack told us about the Berlin Wall. It separates East Berlin from West Berlin. The Communists built it to keep people from leaving East Germany.

After we got off the bus, I said to Eaton, "What's supposed to happen? You keep changing the collage, but I don't see you taking control of Mrs. Bellzack's mind."

"You'll see."

"What do you mean, I'll see?"

"So far I've been trying to get her to identify with the woman in the collage. As soon as she does, I'll have control of her. Then I'll start making her do things. You'll see."

I knew what Eaton was saying. He would try to make Mrs. Bellzack think the collage *was* her, that if the collage woman felt bad, Mrs. Bellzack would too. But something still bothered me.

"How did you know that Mrs. Bellzack would be wearing a green dress today?"

"I didn't."

"But you had to," I said. "You dressed the collage woman in green."

Eaton laughed and said, "If I wanted to, I could probably figure out just what color dress she'll wear. She probably has just a few school outfits and wears them according to some sort of schedule. But I didn't even try to predict what she would wear. I just came prepared."

Then Eaton opened the large cream-colored envelope he was carrying. He took out a handful of paper dresses. Each was a different color. There were even a few striped dresses and one covered with tiny flowers.

"I cut these from magazines and wrapping paper. I can match just about anything Mrs. Bellzack decides to wear."

Eaton is strange, I thought as he walked off to the left and I walked to the right. *But he's smart.* I wondered whether someone as smart as Eaton could really take control of Mrs. Bellzack's mind. And then, what would he do when he had her under his power? *He'd better get me that math award,* I thought.

Six

◆◆◆◆◆◆◆◆◆◆◆

When I got home, Mark was eating doughnuts, tuna fish, pretzels and green peppers. Sometimes I wonder how Mark can eat so much. My parents wonder how they can afford to pay for all that food. Dad even says that when Mark goes to college, it will have to be an out-of-town school, so he eats there and not at home. And the school must have the right kind of meal plan. Dad says that in some schools you pay one price and eat all you want.

"Agha, nagha, nagha," Mark said as I walked past. His mouth was filled with doughnut, and I had no idea what he was saying.

"No thanks," I told him. I figured that "No thanks" is the right answer for just about anything.

I went to my room and looked at the eggs in the incubator. I thought about all those little chicken embryos growing inside those eggs, and I didn't have the heart to break one open.

During the next few days at school, Eaton didn't do much with his mind control experiment. He just kept changing the dresses on the collage woman to match what Mrs. Bellzack was wearing. He made the changes when we left the room for lunch. I kept the log. Sometimes after Mrs. Bellzack looked at the collage, she looked down at what she was wearing. But she never said anything.

We sold our first two history birthday cards. One was for January 27th. The other was for February 10th. After school, Eaton and I went to the library to check what happened on those days.

Eaton knew just where to go. He found a few books which listed what happened in history on each of the 366 days of the year. It's 366 because February 29th was listed too.

On January 27th, Charles Dodgson was born. Most people know him as Lewis Carroll. He wrote *Alice in Wonderland.* Mozart was born on the same day, but a lot of years earlier. Mozart wrote a lot of that old, slow kind of music.

Millard Fillmore, Herbert Hoover and Tom Thumb all were married on February 10th—to three different women. Tom Thumb was a world-famous midget who worked in the circus and met President Lincoln.

I would have made a longer list for those days, but Eaton said that for the one dollar we were charging for the cards, two or three things were enough.

After we left the library, I walked home with Eaton. He was eager to show me his candy-wrapper collection.

As soon as I walked into Eaton's apartment, I met his father. He was sitting at a desk in the hall, working with an adding machine. The one thing I can say about

Eaton's father is that he's neat. There was just one sheet of paper on the desk. Mr. Stanley sat real straight in his chair. He wore a suit, and he has a mustache— a real small, neat one. And he's bald. I'll bet Eaton's father is glad he's bald, because bald is neat. Bald people don't have any hairs out of place.

"Hi, Dad," Eaton said.

"Hmm."

Eaton walked to his room, and I followed him. Now, one thing I can say about Eaton is that he isn't neat.

Clothing was all over the place: on the bed, on the floor and coming out of a few half-opened drawers. There were a few piles of open books. I saw apple cores in some of them. Maybe Eaton uses apple cores as bookmarks. Papers were everywhere.

"Don't you ever clean up?" I asked.

"I just did, yesterday."

Eaton took a shoe box from his closet. He moved some of the clothing off his bed and sat down. Then he opened the box. What was inside looked like garbage to me.

"Look at this," Eaton said as he took out a candy wrapper. "This chocolate was made in Belgium. And this candy was made in Greece."

It looked to me as if it were soaked in grease.

Eaton showed me every sticky wrapper in the box. And he showed me his menus. His mother sends them to him. Eaton said that they aren't stolen. His mother always asks the restaurant manager before she takes one. Eaton was about to show me his ballpoint-pen

collection when I told him I had to go. If I had let him show me his pen collection, I was sure he'd want to show me his pencil, paper-clip and torn-envelope collections. I'm sure he has collections like that. He probably doesn't throw anything out.

In school I kept waiting for Eaton to do something with the collage. All he did was keep changing the collage woman's dress. On the way home from school on Friday, I told Eaton, "If all you plan to do is keep dressing and undressing that picture of yours, then you don't need me to keep a log."

"Just wait," Eaton said. "On Monday the fun starts."

SEVEN

◆◆◆◆◆◆◆◆◆◆◆

Monday morning Eaton was already waiting for the bus when I got to the corner. He didn't say anything. He just patted the cream-colored envelope and smiled.

I sat next to Eaton on the bus. "How was your weekend?" I asked.

Eaton smiled.

"Did you do anything?"

Eaton smiled again.

"Well," I said, "I visited my Aunt Ruth and played with my cousins Jonathan and Michael. And I went ice-skating."

"I didn't," Eaton said. And that was all he said.

When we came to Alice Brenner's house, Alice's mother was standing outside. Mr. Ellman didn't open the door. He didn't want Mrs. Brenner to put her foot in the bus. Then Alice came running out. Mr. Ellman opened the door, and Mrs. Brenner put her foot in.

"Did you eat your breakfast?" Mrs. Brenner asked as Alice came toward the bus.

Alice didn't answer.

"I said, did you eat your breakfast?"

Alice shook her head.

"Then go right back."

Alice went back into the house. Mrs. Brenner still had her foot on the first step of the bus. She turned to Mr. Ellman. She smiled and said, "Breakfast is a very important meal. All the studies show that children need a good breakfast to do well in school."

Mr. Ellman shut off the bus engine. On the floor next to his seat was a newspaper. He picked it up and started to read.

When we got to class, Mrs. Bellzack was already taking attendance. I quickly hung up my coat and sat down.

Mrs. Bellzack was wearing a green dress. I looked at Eaton's collage. The collage woman was wearing a red dress. I knew that Eaton would change her dress during lunch. I wondered what else he would do to the collage woman.

Mrs. Bellzack asked Avi to report on the sales of our history birthday cards. It seemed that they were a real hit. After the two Eaton and I worked on were delivered, we got orders for twelve more.

Avi read off the dates. Then he said, "And please don't write that there was some explosion or that someone died on any of these days. People don't like to know that those things happened on their birthdays. Write upbeat things, like a president was born or some baseball player hit a home run."

Eaton raised his hand.

"Yes, Eaton."

"It seems to me that if there's an explosion or an earthquake on someone's birthday, there's nothing that we can do about it. I mean, the safety pin got its patent on my birthday, and I'm not complaining."

My eyeballs rolled up. I could tell by the way Eaton was talking that if no one stopped him, he would go on for hours.

"Of course," Eaton said, "I would rather it was the cotton gin or the telephone, but what can I do? April 10th is April 10th."

While Eaton caught his breath between sentences, Mrs. Bellzack called on someone else. We had a whole big discussion on what to put on the cards. I agreed with Avi. Lots of things happened in history. We didn't have to list the crummy things that happened on someone's birthday.

Mrs. Bellzack settled the argument. She said that the research committee would have to find five things for every birthday. The card committee would pick the three things they wanted to use.

Sometimes Eaton talks too much. No, not sometimes. Eaton *usually* talks too much. Before he said "April 10th is April 10th," we had to find three things for every day. Now we had to find five.

We had a math lesson next. Then came English. And then came lunch.

As usual, Eaton came into the cafeteria late. I was sitting with Avi and Barry. Eaton sat next to me and began sniffing.

"I smell peanuts," he said.

"I'm eating a peanut-butter sandwich."

"Why?"

"Why? I like peanut butter."

"Did you know that a doctor in St. Louis made the first peanut butter? He made it for patients who needed protein."

"So?"

"Did you know that peanuts are not nuts? They're vegetables."

Barry and Avi changed their seats.

When I finished my "vegetable" sandwich, I took a quick look at Eaton. He was busy with his cream-cheese sandwich. It seemed safe to take out my apple. It wasn't.

"Did you know that there are more than seven thousand kinds of apples?"

Here we go, I thought. *Eaton is going to tell me the names of all seven thousand.*

"About half the world's apples are grown in Europe."

"Eaton, I'm not really interested."

"You should be. You're eating it."

When Eaton wasn't looking, I slipped my little bag of pretzels into my pocket. I didn't want a whole lecture on the history of the pretzel.

The first thing I did when we got back to the room was look at Eaton's collage. He had changed the dress. The collage woman had on a green dress, just like Mrs. Bellzack. And there were three hammers pasted on the collage. They were pounding on the collage woman's head.

I opened the logbook. I wrote:

Procedure: There are hammers pointed at the collage woman's head.

There was a time line of European history on the board. I pretended to be copying the time line. My pencil was moving, but I wasn't writing anything. I was watching Mrs. Bellzack. I wanted to see what would happen when she saw the hammers.

Mrs. Bellzack was still writing on the board, finishing the time line. She was up to 1914.

Maybe she saw it already, I thought. She was in the classroom before we were. *Maybe she saw the green dress and the hammers.*

I waited. Then Mrs. Bellzack turned. She looked to see if we were all copying the time line. She looked straight at me. I was sure she knew that I wasn't copying, but she didn't say anything. She did something at her desk. Then, when Mrs. Bellzack looked at the class again, she saw the collage. I knew she saw it, because she got this funny look on her face. She looked away, to check if we were all working. Then she looked at the collage again—for a long time.

While Mrs. Bellzack taught us about the history of Europe, her eyes kept going back to the collage. I wasn't really listening to what she told us about Europe. I was watching her eyes.

41

Then, in the middle of the lesson, Mrs. Bellzack sat at her desk. She rubbed her forehead. The whole class was watching her. She didn't say anything. She just rubbed her forehead.

"Excuse me for a minute," Mrs. Bellzack said as she got up. She went to her closet and took out a little jar. Aspirin. She took out aspirin.

"I have a headache," she told the class. "Please take out your English readers. Read quietly."

Mrs. Bellzack left the room. She must have gone to the water fountain to take the aspirin.

The hammers did it! They gave Mrs. Bellzack a headache!

EIGHT

◆◆◆◆◆◆◆◆◆◆◆

I took out the logbook. Under *Results,* I wrote:

Mrs. Bellzack got a headache. She took aspirin.

As I wrote the results, I thought that maybe Eaton was a genius. He knows about peanuts and apples, and he can control people's minds. *Imagine that,* I thought. *My friend is a genius.*

On the way home, Eaton wouldn't talk about the experiment, but I could tell he was excited. He was talking about everything else. He told me the proper air pressure for bus tires, the average cost of a new cement-mixer truck and the number of teeth in a wolf's mouth. One of them was fifty-four, I think, but I don't remember which one.

I didn't mind listening to Eaton, not that afternoon.

We decided to meet at the library later—to look up January 22nd, February 2nd, April 8th and March 19th. Those were our days. The other kids on the research committee were looking up the other days.

The next morning at school, Mrs. Bellzack looked at the collage woman a few times. I know she saw the hammers, but I guess they only work once. Mrs. Bellzack rubbed her head a few times, but she didn't say she had a headache, and she didn't take any aspirin.

I wondered what Eaton planned for the afternoon. He had his cream-colored envelope with him.

We had science with Ms. Stanton in the morning. She asked each of us how our experiments were coming along.

"I made an incubator," I told her. "I put in a dozen eggs eleven days ago, and I'm waiting for them to hatch."

"Didn't you plan to break one open every few days to watch the embryos develop?"

"I changed my mind."

"Oh."

"I want to see if the eggs will hatch."

"Well then, in about a week and a half you should have a room full of little chicks."

I hadn't really thought of that.

"Alice," Ms. Stanton said. "How is your experiment coming along?"

"Well, I'm doing an experiment with a plant and the sun."

"What about the plant's daughter?" David called out, but I don't think anyone understood his joke. No one laughed.

"I put a box over a plant," Alice said. "I cut a small window in the box for the sunlight to come in. I'm

44

proving that plants need sun. My plant is bending toward the window."

"What are you doing, Daniel?"

"I'm working with magnets. I'm doing a lot of experiments—like seeing which end is north and which end is south."

"And, Eaton, you haven't told us what you're doing."

"I'm working on something."

"Can you tell us what it is?"

"I'm testing people's reactions to different pictures. I want to see if some pictures can make people happy and others make them sad."

"It's a psychological experiment."

"Sort of."

Why don't you tell her what you're really doing? I thought. Then I knew why. If it worked on Mrs. Bellzack, he could take control of Ms. Stanton's mind too.

Eaton came late to lunch again. I was eating a lettuce and tomato sandwich. Eaton didn't say anything to me about the sandwich. He left Barry and Avi alone too. Eaton just smiled. He smiled throughout lunch. He even laughed once, and no one had said anything funny.

He did something to the collage, I thought, *something funny.* I could hardly wait to get back to class.

NINE

◆◆◆◆◆◆◆◆◆◆◆

As soon as I walked into the room, I looked at the back bulletin board. The collage woman's hair was messed up. It was sticking out and frizzy, like she just got off a motorcycle after a real wild ride.

I knew what Eaton wanted to happen, and it did. As soon as Mrs. Bellzack saw the collage, she touched her hair. Then she opened her closet door and looked in the mirror.

I took out the logbook and wrote:

Procedure: Collage woman's hair is all messed up.
Results: Mrs. Bellzack keeps touching her hair and looking in her mirror.

The lesson was about a hungry people's revolution or something. It happened in 1956. I wasn't listening. I just watched Mrs. Bellzack.

Mrs. Bellzack asked Avi to report on the sales of our history cards. Then she touched her hair again.

"We've sold thirty-eight," Avi said. "There have been a few expenses, for paper and envelopes and things, but we still have more than thirty-five dollars left."

"I think it's time we decided what we should do with the money," Mrs. Bellzack said and touched her hair.

Janet said, "I still think the school needs an elevator, but I don't think thirty-five dollars is enough."

Mrs. Bellzack touched her hair twice while Janet spoke.

"Yes, Barry."

"How about buying a new pen machine? The one in the office never works."

Mrs. Bellzack smoothed her hair down and then called on Daniel.

"I think we should buy a soda machine for the school."

"Susan."

"I thought we needed paper towels, but I saw a girl take about a hundred at once. She said she was watering some plants in her class, and the water spilled. I think we should give the school signs for the bathrooms that say These Towels Are For Drying Wet Hands, Not Wet Floors."

"Eaton."

"The school doesn't own the pen machine in the office. The man who fills it with pens owns it. And soda is not too healthy," Eaton said. "Some sodas have sugar and some sodas have caffeine, so I don't think the school wants a soda machine. I still think we should give the school front pages from old newspapers. There's a place that advertises in one of the magazines I read. They sell copies of famous front pages for just six dollars each. We can frame them and hang them in the halls."

While Eaton spoke, Mrs. Bellzack touched her hair a few times. She even walked to her closet and looked in the mirror once. I think Eaton had more to say, but Mrs. Bellzack stopped him. "Let's take a vote," she said. Then she touched her hair and wrote *Elevator, Pen machine, Soda machine, Towel sign* and *Old newspapers* on the board.

We voted. Eaton's newspaper idea won. It got almost all the votes. Mrs. Bellzack asked Eaton to bring the advertisement to class so she could order the newspaper front pages.

By the end of class, Mrs. Bellzack had touched her hair twenty-three times. *He's done it,* I thought. *Eaton has taken control of Mrs. Bellzack's mind.*

Now's the time, I thought, *to make her schedule a great class trip, like to the "Dandy Duck Cartoon Festival" or to a basketball game. Or maybe Eaton could make Mrs. Bellzack call my parents and tell them what a great kid I am. And he should get her to recommend me for the math award.*

After school, I told all that to Eaton. He shook his head and said, "Not yet. There's a lot more to this experiment. And besides, only a ping-pong would watch Dandy Duck."

I didn't tell Eaton, but I guess I'm a ping-pong. I like that crazy duck. I love it when he flies upside down and says "Watch me quack up."

The next afternoon Eaton changed the collage woman's dress again. He put back the old neat hair. And he surrounded the woman with a desert scene. There was sand, cactus and hot sunlight.

I wondered what Eaton expected to happen. I looked at the collage and tried to imagine that I was the collage woman. I imagined that I was on a hot desert surrounded with sand and cactus, and do you know what? I got thirsty.

Mrs. Bellzack came into the room. She started to talk to us about Poland, something about rye and oats and the things they grow there. Then Mrs. Bellzack saw the collage. I got scared for a minute. She opened her mouth as if she'd swallowed something funny, as if she were gagging. She ran out of the classroom and into the hall. I went to the back door of the room and looked through the little window. Mrs. Bellzack was at the water fountain taking a drink.

It was Wednesday afternoon. When we got off the bus, I said, "Eaton, you have control of Mrs. Bellzack's mind, but you're wasting it."

"What's your problem?"

"I don't have a problem. It's your experiment. All you're doing is making Mrs. Bellzack thirsty and giving her headaches."

"This is science," Eaton said real loud. A woman walking by turned to look at Eaton. "I have no time for your petty Dandy Duck requests. The experiment comes first."

Then Eaton turned the corner and walked home, leaving me and the woman standing there.

"Is he all right?" the woman asked.

"I don't know," I said.

TEN

◆◇◆◇◆◇◆◇◆◇◆

Thursday and Friday I made no entries in the log-book. Eaton didn't do anything. He didn't even change the collage woman's dress. But Monday he did something, something really weird.

When I met him at the bus stop, he didn't have the envelope with him. He had a small cardboard box. And he had a spool of electrical wire. Eaton didn't want me to see the wire, but on the bus it fell out of his pocket. It rolled under the seats ahead of us. I chased after it. I even got yelled at by Mr. Ellman for getting out of my seat while the bus was moving. But when I asked Eaton why he had the wire, he wouldn't tell me.

All morning in class, Eaton didn't say anything. He didn't even raise his hand when we were talking about our senior project.

Eaton didn't line up for lunch with the rest of us. I saved him a seat in the cafeteria, but he never showed up.

After lunch, as soon as I walked into class, I looked

at the back bulletin board. The collage hadn't changed. That worried me.

We're learning about Eastern Europe, and during our social-studies lesson Mrs. Bellzack told us about a trip she took through Hungary. It was about ten years ago, she said, and she went with her parents. The funniest part of the story was when they went for a walk and got lost. They had to catch a train, and no one understood them when they asked where the train station was. Finally her mother went up to people and said, "Choo, choo, chuga, chuga, chuga." The first few people walked away real fast, as though there were something wrong with her mother. Then someone laughed and pointed to the station. It was only two blocks away.

While Mrs. Bellzack told her story, I looked over at Eaton a few times. Every time I looked at him, he smiled.

Our math lesson was next. It was on changing decimals to fractions. It's not too hard, and Mrs. Bellzack didn't waste much time trying to make us understand what we were doing. She just told us how to do it.

Then it happened. Mrs. Bellzack wrote *Homework* on the board. She underlined it, and she began to write the first problem.

Bzzz.

"What's that noise?" Janet asked.

Mrs. Bellzack stopped writing, and the noise stopped.

Mrs. Bellzack looked around. Then she started to write a second problem.

Bzzz. Bzzz.

"Stop it," Susan said. "I'm getting a headache."

Every time Mrs. Bellzack wrote a homework problem, the buzzing started. A few kids screamed, but no one knew what was making the sound. When Mrs. Bellzack stopped writing, the buzzing stopped. She usually gives us ten or twelve math problems for homework. That day she gave us only four.

The second time I heard the buzzing, I looked over at Eaton. He had his hand in his pocket. And then I saw something really strange. There was an electrical wire which went from his pants leg to the door of our coat closet.

"Well," Eaton asked when we got on the bus, "what do you think? I've really got that Bellzack under my control."

"I thought you didn't want to talk about it on the bus," I whispered.

"You're right."

We came to Alice Brenner's stop. Her mother was standing in the street again. Eaton pointed to Mrs. Brenner and whispered, "Maybe I'll take control of her mind next."

We got off the bus, and Eaton asked me, "Have you ever heard of Ivan Petrovich Pavlov?"

"No."

"He was a Russian scientist. He did experiments with dogs. He gave me the idea for my homework

buzzer. Every time she begins to write something on the board that I don't like, I'll give her the buzz."

"She gave us less homework today."

"That's right. And I've been reading about a guy named Franz Anton Mesmer. Wait till you see what I do tomorrow."

When I got home, I asked Mark if he knew anything about Mesmer. Mark told me he was a skinny football player who was always getting tackled. I didn't think that was the Mesmer Eaton was talking about, so I went to the library.

I had heard the word *mesmerized.* Well, it came from this guy Mesmer. He lived in the seventeen- and eighteen-hundreds, and he discovered hypnosis.

So that's what Eaton planned to do, to hypnotize Mrs. Bellzack. I once saw a man hypnotized on a TV show. Every time a bell rang, he clucked like a chicken. I wondered what Eaton would make Mrs. Bellzack do. I closed my eyes and imagined her clucking. Then, when I imagined Mrs. Bellzack crawling on the floor and barking like a dog, I started to laugh. I couldn't stop.

"Shhh," someone in the library said. "I'm trying to work."

"Young man," someone else said. I opened my eyes and saw the librarian. "Please stop your laughing. You're disturbing the other patrons."

I closed the book about Mesmer and left the library. I wondered how Eaton planned to hypnotize Mrs. Bellzack.

ELEVEN

◆◆◆◆◆◆◆◆◆◆◆

The next morning at the bus stop, Eaton showed me a shiny silver pendant. He told me to relax and look at the pendant while he twirled it.

"I know what you're trying to do," I told Eaton. "You want to mesmerize me. But I'm not going to let you."

Eaton put the pendant in his pocket.

"What are you going to make Mrs. Bellzack do?" I whispered. "Are you going to make her cluck or bark or growl?"

"No. I'm going to make her scratch like a monkey. Every time I say the word *frog* she's going to scratch."

As soon as we walked into class, Eaton went to Mrs. Bellzack's desk. He had brought in the magazine advertisement for the front pages from old newspapers. While he was up there, I saw him take the pendant from his pocket and whisper something to Mrs. Bellzack. It was probably "You are getting sleepy. Your eyes are getting heavy." Or something like that.

During class, Eaton had his hand raised almost all

the time. During the math lesson, Mrs. Bellzack asked, "What is the fractional equivalent of .03?"

She called on Eaton.

He said, "Three one-hundredths, frog."

As soon as Eaton said "Frog," Mrs. Bellzack scratched herself. She scratched with her right hand under her left arm. It wasn't really like a monkey, but maybe she doesn't know how a monkey scratches.

During our literature lesson, Eaton said the author of *Tom Sawyer* was Mark "Frog" Twain. And Mrs. Bellzack scratched again.

After lunch during our social-studies lesson, Eaton raised his hand and said, "The real name of Hungary is Hungarian People's Republic. Their dollar is called a forint. Frog." And Mrs. Bellzack scratched.

When Mrs. Bellzack wrote *Homework* on the board, Eaton's buzzer sounded. Janet screamed. Mrs. Bellzack started to write the assignment, and Eaton buzzed again. Janet screamed again. Then Mrs. Bellzack turned to face the class. She said, "You know what. Today I won't give any homework." A few kids said "Thank you" to Mrs. Bellzack. They should have thanked Eaton.

When we got off the bus that afternoon, Eaton said, "Now that I'm sure I have Mrs. Bellzack under my control, what would you like her to do?"

"I want to win the sixth-grade math prize."

"I'll do that next week. How about if I get Mrs. Bellzack to call your parents and tell them how great you're doing in school?"

Eaton didn't wait for me to answer. He just started

walking real fast. I had to run to keep up with him. Then, at the corner, he turned right instead of left.

"Where are you going?"

"To your house. I'll need a picture of you and your parents."

Eaton knew just where I lived. He had never been to my house before, and I had never told him my address. Maybe, when he's bored with reading encyclopedias, he reads telephone books. Maybe he knows *everyone's* address.

When we came in, Mark was eating his favorite sandwich, butter and cinnamon on rye.

"Do you know what you're eating?" Eaton asked. "You're eating fat and tree bark."

"What?"

"Butter is made from milk fat, and cinnamon is made from the bark of the cinnamon laurel tree."

"Who is this kid?" Mark asked me.

"His name is Eaton. He's a friend of mine."

"Agha, nagha, nagha," Mark said. He had a mouthful of his fat and bark sandwich.

"No thanks," I said as I walked with Eaton to my room.

"You understood him?"

"Sure," I said. But of course I didn't.

Eaton walked real slowly around my room. Then he looked under my bed, behind my night table and in my closet.

"All right," he said after he closed the closet door, "where do you keep all your collections and other junk?"

I showed him my wastepaper basket and said, "This is where I keep my junk."

Eaton rolled his eyeballs back and said, "Weird, just like my father."

I showed Eaton my incubator. He looked through the window for a really long time. Then he said, "You better start buying chicken feed. These eggs look about ready to hatch."

I'm sure he made that up. How could Eaton tell if an egg is about to hatch?

I showed Eaton the box of family photographs that Mom keeps. He looked at them real slowly, as though he was studying them. While he was looking, he said, "You were a cute baby. What happened?"

Eaton picked out a photograph of me and one of my parents. Then he said he had to get home. He was expecting a package of menus from his mother.

At the door Eaton told me, "I'm going to put a telephone in the collage woman's hand and a big smile on her face. And where her eyes are, I'm going to paste the pictures of you and your parents. She'll probably call your parents tomorrow night. She'll probably tell them good things about your work."

After Eaton left, I thought about what he planned to do. I remembered that he said she'd "probably" say good things about my work. Suddenly I wasn't too sure about having my picture on Eaton's collage.

TWELVE

◆◇◆◇◆◇◆◇◆◇◆

The next morning while we were waiting for the bus, I told Eaton not to use my picture.

"We'll talk about it," he said.

"When?"

Just then the bus came. "We can't talk about it now," Eaton whispered as we got on the bus.

I had the window seat. Eaton sat next to me.

"Why not?" I whispered.

"I don't want anyone to hear us. I don't want anyone to know about the experiment."

That's just like Eaton. He didn't want anyone to know about *his* collage. But he was pasting *my* picture on it.

I looked at Eaton's books. He was carrying his notebook, social-studies book and volume fifteen of some encyclopedia. My picture was probably inside that cream-colored envelope of his. I didn't see the envelope. I knew Eaton had it with him. It was probably inside his notebook. I decided that as we got off the bus, I would grab his notebook and take out the envelope.

The front door to Alice's house was open when we got there. Mr. Ellman stopped the bus. He opened the door when someone with long blonde hair came out. She looked like Alice. She was carrying an armload of books and walking real quickly, with her head down. She put one foot in the bus and then looked up. It was Mrs. Brenner.

"Alice will be right out," she said.

"Start driving," someone yelled from the back of the bus. "She'll take her foot out."

"That woman has some nerve," a girl sitting in the front said.

Mrs. Brenner stepped onto the bus. She walked toward the girl and said, "Don't talk to me about nerve."

As soon as Mrs. Brenner walked onto the bus, Mr. Ellman released the brake. He was about to drive off when Mrs. Brenner realized what was happening. She quickly got off the bus—all except one foot.

We waited almost five minutes for Alice to come out. When we got to school, everyone rushed to get off the bus. A whole bunch of kids got between me and Eaton, and I couldn't grab the notebook.

When we got to class, mean Mrs. Cannon was standing there with her arms folded. "You'll all be quiet now," she yelled, "or I'll be in touch with your parents." Mrs. Cannon was working as a reading teacher this year. She had no class for the first hour. She patrolled the halls and watched the classes of teachers who came late.

The only real noise in the room was the clicking of

Mrs. Cannon's shoes as she walked around the class. She had this real mean scowl on her face as she passed my desk. I followed her with my eyes. And then I saw it—Eaton's collage.

He had come on the bus with me, so I didn't know when he had done it, but what he had done was strange. The collage woman's face was all scratched and bandaged. She was holding a steering wheel, and behind her was a picture of two cars crashing.

Mrs. Cannon banged her ruler on the desk. "Class," she said, "your teacher has been delayed. Take a book out and read quietly."

As I reached for my social-studies book, I looked over at Eaton. He was reading his encyclopedia. I made faces at him to get his attention.

"Young man," Mrs. Cannon told me, "try to look normal."

I opened my social-studies book, but I didn't read it. I kept thinking about that collage. *When did Eaton change it?*

Just then the door opened, and Mrs. Bellzack walked in. She looked horrible. She was scratched and dirty. There were bandages on her face. I looked back at the collage. The bandages on Mrs. Bellzack were in the same places as the ones on the collage woman!

The two teachers spoke for a few minutes. Then Mrs. Bellzack said, "Don't worry. I'm fine," and Mrs. Cannon left.

Mrs. Bellzack dropped her books on her desk and sat down. "Just give me a minute to get myself to-

gether," she told the class. "I had a slight problem with my car this morning, and I'm still a little upset."

I knew what her problem was. She had had an accident. And it was all Eaton's fault. He pasted the accident on the collage. He made it happen.

I looked over at Eaton. He was still calmly reading his encyclopedia. *How can he be so cold and cruel?* I coughed. He didn't look up. I coughed again, louder and longer. Just about the whole class looked at me, including Eaton.

I mouthed the words "Why did you do it?"

Eaton gave me a funny look, like he didn't know what I was saying.

I pointed to the collage woman. Eaton turned and looked at it. Then he shook his head and shrugged his shoulders, like he didn't know how it all had happened.

I didn't listen much to the class lessons that morning. I was too upset.

When it was time for lunch, I got in line. But Eaton didn't. I knew where he was. He was inside changing the collage again. *Hasn't he had enough?* I asked myself.

A short while later, Eaton sat next to me in the cafeteria. When he sat down, Barry and Avi got up and moved to another table. I was eating a peanut-butter sandwich, but Eaton didn't say anything to me about the peanut smell.

"Why did you do it?" I asked.
"Do what?"

"You know what. Why did you make Mrs. Bellzack have an accident?"

"I didn't paste those cars and bandages on the collage. And anyway, a collage can't cause an accident."

"It's your collage and your experiment. You're responsible," I said, and as I said it, the bottom slice of bread fell off my sandwich. I put the bread back. With tuna fish or egg salad, it would have been a problem. But not with peanut butter. The bread stuck right on.

"You're getting hysterical," Eaton told me.

"You think this is funny!"

"I don't mean hysterical ha-ha. I mean hysterical ding-dong, cuckoo."

"If your collage can make Mrs. Bellzack thirsty and give her a headache, why couldn't it cause an accident?"

"I don't know," Eaton said, and for the first time, he didn't sound so sure of himself. "This whole thing is beginning to worry me. Somehow that collage changed, but I didn't do it. And the collage is not working the way it's supposed to. Mrs. Bellzack had her car accident *before* she saw the collage. Now, maybe you can explain *that* to me!"

I couldn't.

After we finished eating, Eaton told me not to worry about the collage. He had taken off the crashing cars and the bandages. He said he had put on my photographs and a telephone, and a nice big smile on the collage woman's face.

"How could you do that!"

"With paste."

"No. How could you paste my picture on the collage? You said you wouldn't."

"All I said is that we'd talk about it. If you want, we can talk about it now."

" 'Now' is too late," I told Eaton as we walked back to class. "And if she calls my parents and gives a bad report, I'm telling Mrs. Bellzack that you've been playing with her head."

Eaton didn't say anything to that.

I knew Eaton was a know-it-all, but I didn't think he was a liar. But there it was! When I came into the room, the collage was real different, not like Eaton said it would be. My photographs weren't on it. The collage woman wasn't smiling. She had this really angry look on her face, and her hair was dripping wet.

I knew what would happen. And it did. When Mrs. Bellzack came into the room, her hair was wet, and she didn't look happy.

"What happened to your hair?" Susan asked.

"What do you think happened!" Mrs. Bellzack said, and she shook her head. Water sprayed off her hair. "It got wet."

She went to her closet, took out a towel and dried her hair.

I looked over at Eaton. He was moving his mouth, trying to tell me something. It was either "Frogs under umbrella fish" or "Freckles and belly gosh." I'm not sure which. I'm not very good at lip reading.

I shrugged my shoulders and turned my hands

palms up to let Eaton know that I had no idea what he was saying.

Eaton wrote a note and passed it to Jenny Hunt. She tossed it onto my desk. It said, "Someone changed the collage! I didn't give the woman wet hair!!!!"

There were four exclamation points after *hair*.

It was hard to believe Eaton, but it was also hard not to believe four exclamation points. I mean, why would he tell me he didn't make the collage woman's hair wet? And if he didn't do it, who did?

I don't really remember what happened during the rest of the afternoon. I didn't pay much attention to the lessons. And on the bus, I was in such a daze I almost missed my stop. Eaton had to poke me. I kept thinking about that collage.

"If you're not changing the collage, who is?" I asked Eaton as we got off the bus.

"I don't know," he said. "But I've read science-fiction stories about inanimate objects that come to life."

Then Eaton said to me in that I-know-more-than-you-do tone of his, "*Inanimate* means not living."

"Oh, really?" I said. "I thought inanimate was an explosive."

"No. You're confusing inanimate with dynamite."

I wasn't confusing anything. I was joking. But you can't joke around with Eaton Stanley.

At the corner, just before Eaton turned left and I turned right, he said, "I think maybe it's time to take the collage down. I've done enough experimenting. I'll take it down during lunch tomorrow."

This business about the collage coming to life scared me. I was glad Eaton was going to take it down. I thought we were finished with Eaton's collage and his mind control experiment.

We weren't.

THIRTEEN
◆◆◆◆◆◆◆◆◆◆◆

The next morning we were late again. We had to wait for Alice Brenner. When we walked in, Mrs. Cannon was standing in front of the class.

"Well, look who's here," she said. "Goldilocks and her two beaus."

When she said that, Eaton pinched his nose, as if he smelled something bad. He did that because *beau* means a girl's sweetheart and Eaton wanted everyone in the class to know that he wasn't in love with Alice "Goldilocks" Brenner.

I didn't pinch my nose or anything. I just sat in my seat. Then I had a horrible thought. *The last time Mrs. Cannon came to our class, the collage had caused a car accident.* I wondered if the collage had caused Mrs. Bellzack to be late again.

I put my hand in front of my face and turned just a little. I looked through my fingers at the collage.

She was in a house which was surrounded with flames!

I jumped out of my seat.

"Where are you going, young man?" Mrs. Cannon asked.

"I have to leave the room. It's an emergency."

"I'm terribly sorry, young man. But I don't allow emergencies. In my class, everyone stays seated."

"But . . ."

"Goats butt. Children sit."

I sat in my seat. *At this very moment,* I thought, *Mrs. Bellzack's house might be burning. Somehow I have to call the fire department or the police or someone.*

I looked over at Eaton. He shrugged his shoulders and turned his hands palms up, as though he didn't know what to do. *For a know-it-all, Eaton certainly doesn't know it all,* I thought.

I knew that I had to do something. I couldn't just sit there. I got up again.

"Sit," Mrs. Cannon commanded, as though I were her pet dog.

"I can't sit. There's an emergency," I said.

I opened the door just as Mrs. Bellzack walked in. "You're safe," I said. "You're safe."

"Of course I'm safe," Mrs. Bellzack said as she rushed past me. "I'm just a little late."

Mrs. Bellzack hung up her coat and spoke to Mrs. Cannon. I noticed Mrs. Cannon point to me as she talked.

Mrs. Bellzack looked just fine to me. *Maybe there wasn't any fire,* I thought.

After Mrs. Cannon left, Mrs. Bellzack said, "I'd like

71

to talk for a few minutes about fire prevention. What should we all do to prevent fires?"

I knew it. There had been a fire and Eaton and his collage were responsible. I felt responsible too, because I knew what was happening, and I wasn't doing anything about it.

"You can prevent fires by not smoking in bed," Susan said.

Mrs. Bellzack smiled and said, "Yes, don't smoke in bed. And if you want to prevent heart and lung disease, don't smoke at all."

"Don't overload your sockets," Janet said.

"Make sure matches are out before you throw them away."

"Don't play with matches."

"Keep papers and things away from the stove."

I wanted to say, "Don't let Eaton make a collage," but I didn't.

We talked for a long time about fires and what to do about them. The best thing to do is to call the fire department and not to try to put them out yourself. I already knew that.

All morning I thought about Eaton's collage and all the trouble it had caused. I was glad he was taking it down at lunch.

When Eaton came into the cafeteria later, he was smiling. "Well," he said as he sat next to me, "that's the end of the experiment. I took the collage down. It's in my notebook now."

"Did you notice anything funny about the collage? I mean, can you tell how it came to life?"

"Those flames were pasted on. Here," he said as he reached into his pocket. "I tore one off."

The flame had been torn from a magazine. I could tell because on the back of it was an advertisement for hemorrhoid medicine.

"If the collage had come to life," I said, "there wouldn't be hemorrhoids on the back of the flames."

"That's what I thought," Eaton said. "Someone has been playing with my experiment."

"Why are you whispering?" I asked, and Eaton told me to turn around. Barry and Avi were standing there.

"Do you know anything about the picture on the back bulletin board that keeps changing?" Avi asked.

"No," Eaton said, "but I do know about perfumes. Some are made from a gland in the stomach of a musk deer. People kill the deer and take out the gland."

"Just so people can smell good?" I asked. "That sounds barbaric. Why don't people just take baths?"

"What about that picture?" Barry asked. "And why do you always come late to lunch?"

"Would you like to know how many eggs a mother herring lays?"

Just then the bell rang. Lunch was over. As we walked to class, Avi said, "Are you going to answer us or not?"

"Sure," Eaton said as we walked into the room. "A herring can lay thirty thousand or more eggs at one time."

I wondered who else had noticed the collage. And I wondered if anyone thought that I had something to do with it.

I didn't even look at the bulletin board. We were having a math lesson, so I copied the problems off the board.

Then I heard a cough, a long and loud cough. It was Eaton. He was trying to get my attention. When I turned to look at him, he pointed to the back bulletin board.

The collage was there! And there were pictures of books falling on the collage woman's head.

I wanted to believe that Eaton had taken the collage down. But how could he have taken it down if it was still there?

Maybe Barry and Avi are changing the collage, I thought. But then I realized it couldn't be them. They always walked down to lunch with the rest of the class.

All through math, I waited for the books to fall. But they didn't. Then Mrs. Bellzack talked to us about Shakespeare. He lived about four hundred years ago, and Mrs. Bellzack called him the greatest playwright of all time.

"Let me read to you from some of his writings," she said. She reached for a book on the top shelf in the book closet, and then it happened. Two books fell. One hit her right on the head, and the class laughed. Mrs. Bellzack didn't laugh. And neither did Eaton or I.

Mrs. Bellzack read to us from one of Shakespeare's plays, *Measure for Measure*. From Act Two she read, "Oh, it is excellent to have a giant's strength; but it is tyrannous to use it like a giant."

She's talking about us, I thought. *Mind control is a giant's strength. And we're using it like an evil giant!*

She read to us from *The Merry Wives of Windsor,* "Better three hours too soon than a minute too late." *If we're going to help her, we should do it soon.*

Then she read from Act Three of *Measure for Measure,* "The miserable have no other medicine, but only hope."

She's miserable, I thought. *And she hopes someone will save her.*

"I'll save you," I called out. "I'll save you!"

The whole class laughed. They thought I was joking.

"I don't have to be saved," Mrs. Bellzack said. She was smiling. "But thank you, Brian."

She thought I was joking too.

But I wasn't. Mrs. Bellzack was in great danger. Eaton's collage woman had already caused a car accident, a fire and a falling Shakespeare. I was afraid to even think about what might be next.

FOURTEEN

◇◇◇◇◇◇◇◇◇◇◇

"I put the collage in my notebook," Eaton said as we walked to the bus. "I left the notebook on my desk when I went to lunch. When I came back, the note-book was there, but the collage wasn't. It was on the bulletin board."

"We have to do something about it," I told Eaton on the bus.

"I have a plan," Eaton whispered. "We'll catch the person who's changing the collage. I'll tell you about it when we get off the bus."

When we got off the bus, Eaton whispered, "Tomor-row both of us will hide in the room. We'll just wait, and when we hear someone come into the room, we'll both jump out and surprise him."

Eaton told me where he'd been hiding—behind the coats. "It's a great spot," Eaton said. "If the coat is long enough, even my feet don't show."

When I came home, Mark was eating. I think it was a tuna and salami sandwich, but I'm not sure.

"Agha, nagha, nagha," Mark said as I walked past.

"No thanks."

"AGHA, NAGHA, NAGHA," he said again, but louder.

I didn't think "No thanks" was the right answer this time. I waited for him to swallow.

"Don't open the door to your room," he said.

"What?"

"Well, you can open the door to your room, but don't leave it open."

"Why not?"

"You'll see," Mark said and he smiled funny. Then he bit into his sandwich again.

I didn't wait for Mark to swallow. I slowly opened the door to my room. Everything was the way I had left it in the morning. *Just another one of Mark's jokes,* I thought. I threw my books on the bed, took off my shoes and lay down.

Peep.

The sound was so small, I almost didn't hear it.

Peep.

I heard it again.

I looked over the edge of my bed and saw a tiny, scrawny chick run past. Then I saw another. They were all over the place. I saw one run out the door. "Oh, no," I yelled and ran after it. I followed the chick into the kitchen.

"I told you to close the door," Mark said. It was pointless to ask Mark to help me. He was still eating.

I caught the chick under the table. It was so small, all feather and bone. I carefully carried it into my

PEEP
PEEP

room. With one hand, I opened my sock drawer, dumped out the socks and put the chick in.

There were still seven eggs in the incubator. That meant five had hatched.

I looked under my bed. I saw two chicks, but they were beyond my reach. I ran to the other side of the bed. But the chicks had moved. I still couldn't reach them. I rolled a pair of socks toward the chicks. They ran to get out of the way of the rolling socks, and I caught them both. I gently put the two chicks into my sock drawer.

Two more to go.

I looked under my desk, in my closet and behind my night table. *Peep.* The sound came from the hallway. I ran out of my room and saw the chick run into the bathroom. *Maybe it has to go,* I thought. I ran after it and caught it behind the toilet.

One more to catch.

I looked in the bathroom, under my parents' beds and in their closets. I even put my ear to the ground and listened for the sound of tiny feet running. I didn't hear any sounds. I looked in the living room, and when I didn't know where else to look, I went into the kitchen. Mark was holding the chick.

"I've been looking all over for that chick!"

"Well, here it is," Mark said. "And I think it could use a drink of water."

I took the chick from Mark. I put it in the drawer with the others. Then I filled two small paper cups with water and put them in the drawer too.

I looked through the window of the incubator.

There were still seven eggs inside. Then I realized that even if another one of the eggs did hatch, the chick couldn't get out.

"Hey, Mark," I said as I walked into the kitchen, "how did those chicks get out of the incubator?"

"I let them out. It seemed cruel to leave them *peeping* away inside those boxes."

I guess he was right. I sat on one of the kitchen chairs to rest.

"What do you plan to do with all those chicks?" Mark asked.

"I don't know."

"But you knew they were going to hatch."

"They weren't due until tomorrow."

"Well," Mark said, "maybe they don't have calendars inside their tiny eggs. Anyway, what were you going to do with them tomorrow?"

I sat there for a long time, just thinking. Mark watched me. "What are you looking at?" I asked.

Mark got up and went to the refrigerator. He took out a bowl of cold tuna casserole. "Do you know what I would do?" Mark asked between nibbles of the casserole. "I'd take the chicks to the farm where Dad bought the eggs."

"That's it!" I said. I called Dad. When I told him that the eggs had hatched, he came right home. Then he drove me to the farm. I sat in the back seat with the chicks on my lap and the incubator next to me.

The man at the farm laughed when I told him what had happened. He was happy to take the chicks. He also took the fertile eggs that hadn't hatched and put them in his own incubator.

"This should teach you a lesson," my father said as we drove home.

"What's the lesson?"

" 'Don't count your chickens before they hatch,' " my father said. "No, that's not it. How about 'The race is not always to the swift'?"

He was teasing me. When I was young, Dad read Aesop's fables to me. And at the end of each fable, there was always a moral, as if everything that happens in life should teach some great lesson.

" 'Only fools try to use new tools.' 'Look before you leap.' Or 'It is best to be prepared.' "

"I think I have it," I said. " 'If you don't own a chicken farm, don't build an incubator.' "

My room was a mess. I straightened it and thought again about hiding behind some coats tomorrow and catching whoever is changing the collage. And I wondered what lesson I should learn from Eaton's mind control experiment.

FIFTEEN

◇◆◇◆◇◆◇◆◇◆◇

The next morning I told Eaton about the chicks.

"Do you know that there is more protein in a cup of roasted peanuts than in a cup of chicken à la king?"

"Eaton," I said, "I don't want a whole lesson on chicken facts."

"There's more protein in a cooked chicken than in an egg. Now explain that to me! If a chicken comes out of an egg, where does the extra protein come from?"

I rolled my eyeballs up.

The bus stopped. We were in front of Alice Brenner's house. Mr. Ellman must have been dreaming, because he opened the bus door without even looking to see if Alice was ready. And, of course, she wasn't. But Mrs. Brenner was. She put one foot in the bus and smiled at the driver.

Suddenly Mr. Ellman realized where he was and what was happening. "You can't keep doing this," he said. "Tomorrow I'm not going to stop here."

"You have to stop. I pay my taxes."

Just then Alice ran out of the house. She was holding her books and drinking her soft-boiled eggs. Alice ran onto the bus. As Alice gave her mother the paper cup, the bottom fell out, and egg splattered all over the front of Alice's coat.

"Look what you did! You go right in and change. The bus will wait," Mrs. Brenner said. But she had taken her foot out of the bus.

Alice got off the bus. As she did, Mr. Ellman closed the door. Mrs. Brenner banged on the side of the bus. She was screaming something as the bus drove off, but I couldn't hear her. The bus windows were closed.

Everyone cheered. And while the bus waited at a red light, Mr. Ellman stood up. He was really smiling. He turned to all of us and took a deep bow, like he was a great actor.

We got to school early, and Eaton tried to get upstairs to take down the collage, but he couldn't. There was a teacher standing at every door.

When we got up to class, Mrs. Bellzack wasn't there. Mrs. Cannon was standing in the front of the room. She was banging a ruler against the teacher's desk and yelling, "Hurry! Be seated! No talking!"

As I walked to my seat, I looked at the back bulletin board, and I knew why Mrs. Bellzack was late. She had broken her arm. The collage woman's left arm was in a cast.

I sat at my desk with my head down. *We broke her arm now,* I thought. *Eaton and his stupid collage broke her arm.*

"Hey, Sleeping Beauty, wake up," Mrs. Cannon said.

Jenny poked me in the back. I looked up. Mrs. Cannon was talking to me. She was calling *me* Sleeping Beauty.

I looked over at Eaton. He was shaking his head, letting me know that it wasn't his idea to break Mrs. Bellzack's arm.

I opened my notebook and wrote a note for Eaton. I folded it and gave it to Jenny. She tossed it to Eaton.

SWAT!

Mrs. Cannon smacked the desk with her ruler. "Bring me that note," she said.

Jenny picked up the note and took it to Mrs. Cannon.

"Well," Mrs. Cannon said as she opened the note, "let's see what our Sleeping Beauty has written to his Frog Prince."

Then Mrs. Cannon read from the note, " 'We have to tell her. We can't wait until lunch.' "

Just then the door opened. Mrs. Bellzack walked in. Her left arm was in a plaster cast. I was about to walk up to Mrs. Bellzack and tell her "It's our fault. It's our fault you broke your arm," when I felt someone pull on my pants leg. It was Eaton. He had crawled along the floor to my desk.

"Don't tell her yet," Eaton whispered. "At least give me a chance to catch whoever is changing the collage."

I watched as Eaton crawled back to his seat.

I looked at Mrs. Bellzack. Mark broke his arm once, and it really hurt. I felt sorry for Mrs. Bellzack, but I didn't run up and tell her it was my fault. I was afraid to with mean Mrs. Cannon standing there. And it wasn't my fault anyway. That broken arm was either Eaton's fault or whoever pasted that cast on the collage.

When it was time for lunch, I hid behind a long blue coat. I don't know whose coat it was, but it smelled.

At first, as everyone was getting their lunch bags and leaving the room, it was noisy. Then I heard the door close and lock. I had a real eerie feeling hiding behind that coat. The room was *so* quiet.

"Eaton, Eaton, are you there?"

No one answered.

"EATON."

There was still no answer. Then I heard a noise. Someone was unlocking the door. I waited. I heard the door open.

"Aha, now I've caught you!"

That was Eaton. I pushed the coat aside to see who he had caught.

Mrs. Bellzack was standing there. "Shouldn't you two be in the cafeteria now?" she asked.

That's when I told her everything, about the experiment, the logbook—and that we were responsible for the fire, the car accident and her broken arm.

"I don't think you have the right to control me," Mrs. Bellzack said. "I don't think anyone has."

"All I wanted to do," Eaton said, "was make you thirsty and give you headaches and things. Then the collage began changing by itself. I lost control of it, and those terrible things began to happen."

"Eaton," Mrs. Bellzack said, "did you really think

I didn't notice that you were never in line for lunch? Did you really think you could hypnotize me?"

Eaton didn't answer.

"And you, Brian. I didn't know you were involved until I saw your picture on the collage. Really! I thought you had better sense."

I didn't say anything either.

Then Mrs. Bellzack smiled. "I didn't break my arm," she said, and she took the cast off. It was fake. One side was plaster, and the other side had elastic bands to keep it on.

"What about the car accident?" I asked.

"And the wet hair? And the fire?" Eaton asked.

"There was no car accident. I changed the collage myself. There wasn't any fire either. My hair *was* wet, but I did that. At the beginning of your experiment, you had fun watching me. You thought you gave me a headache and made me thirsty. At the end, I had fun watching you."

"Did my experiment work at all?" Eaton asked.

"No," Mrs. Bellzack said. "I just wanted to teach you boys a lesson. You have enough to do to take care of yourselves. I don't think you're ready to take control of someone else."

We just stood there for a while. She didn't say anything, and neither did we. *Now comes the punishment,* I thought. And it did.

"You know, boys," Mrs. Bellzack said, "since you have such a great interest in mind control, I think it would be a good idea for you to write a report on it. It should be at least thirty pages."

Because of Eaton, I thought, *I'll spend the next few weeks reading encyclopedias and writing.*

"And boys, since you don't seem to need a full lunch period, you'll help me patrol the halls."

I thought Eaton would apologize for getting me into such a mess of trouble. He didn't.

"Did you know," he asked me when we sat down in the cafeteria, "that there are thousands of different kinds of rice?"

I didn't answer him.

"Did you know that not all cow's milk tastes the same? It depends on what the cow eats. And horses sleep standing up."

I didn't say anything.

"We'll need extra time to do that report. So you know what? I have a plan to change the school's bell schedule. I'll change the clock that rings the bells by just a few minutes each day. By the end of three weeks, we'll be getting out an hour earlier every day."

"Really!" I said. "If I get home just a half hour earlier, I can watch the Dandy Duck show. It's on at two-thirty."

"You really do like that crazy duck, don't you," Eaton said. "Well, you can make a date to watch him next Thursday."